CW01497977

Warning

This book contains scenes that some people may find disturbing, including scenes of gory violence and sexual violence. This book is intended for an adult audience and may not be suitable for some people. Reader discretion is advised.

This book is a work of fiction.

Disclaimer

If, at any time while reading this book, you feel the need to shout, "But that's not how the human body works!" I'd like to offer you my sincerest apologies. Most regrettably, I couldn't get my hands on a living human subject to experiment on.

Acknowledgment

Many thanks to Lyndie Lei, Christina, and Carrington for letting me slaughter them violently.

1. The Predator

Alex DeMembre wasn't like the other girls. She was much, much worse. That, and the fact that at twenty-nine years old, she wasn't a girl at all, but a woman.

Ever since rumors of a serial killer operating near her town had spread, she'd been on the lookout for him. She hadn't believed it at first; after all, to her knowledge, there had only been three serial killers in Switzerland—four if you counted Thomas Sebert, but he hadn't really acted long enough to meet the criteria. So the odds of a new one emerging now, right next to her home, were close to absolute zero.

Then, mutilated bodies began to pile up, and she caught herself hoping. She had carefully studied all the information that had been shared with the general public about the man known as the Geneva Mangler, as well as security recommendations. This Friday night, for the fifth night in a row, she was about to merrily ignore them all.

She slipped on a black lace crop top that barely concealed her ample bosom, a short skirt made of dark red tulle, and black fishnet suspenders. She combed her long, curly black hair, added smoky eyeliner and bloodred lipstick. Satisfied with her appearance, she left the house and headed, alone, for the area where most of the disappearances had taken place. Her heart was beating fiercely, and a sweet warmth was spreading through her lower belly at the thought that this night might be the night—the one when her wildest dreams would come true.

Her chest contracted as she walked into the dark alley, lighted only by a flickering streetlamp. What if he came? What if he didn't? She paced back and forth anxiously, a million thoughts racing through her mind. Footsteps sounded behind her, making her jump, and she turned around to see a menacing silhouette approaching.

"Well, well, well, look at what we have here. Don't you know it's not safe to wander around all on your own, especially for a pretty little thing like you?"

Alex's heart missed a beat, her breath catching in her chest.

"Are you the Geneva Mangler?" she whispered.

"In the flesh." The man grinned, his deep voice causing her to shiver. "And it's too late for you to escape now, doll."

"I don't want to escape," she breathed, swallowing hard. "I wanted to meet you."

"Meet me?" The man chuckled, looking genuinely amused. "Yes, I've heard about this before: serial killers getting strings of love letters in prison. You're a hybristophiliac, aren't you? A willing victim . . . Yes, it could be fun. Tell me, sweetheart, would you like me to show you what I can do?"

His cold blue eyes bore into her, almost hypnotic. She couldn't believe everything was going so well. It was perfect.

"Yes. That's exactly what I want." Her voice seemed distant to her own ears. Everything seemed so surreal.

"Let's make a deal, then. From now on, you belong to me, body and soul. I can use you however I like, and I don't care whether you like it or not. I'll eventually kill you when I so choose. In exchange, I'll unveil sensations you can't even imagine, and I promise you that your death will be memorable." He held out his hand, a sadistic challenge glinting in his eyes.

Alex bit her lip. She could tell he expected her to change her mind and panic, but he was wrong. This was everything she'd ever hoped for and more. She didn't care if she died tonight, as long as it was slow, painful, and erotic.

"Deal," she answered, shaking his hand.

The man frowned but didn't falter, the corner of his mouth soon stretching into a sinister smile. He motioned for her to follow him to his black Porsche and drove to a large, somewhat isolated house on the edge of town.

Alex studied him carefully. He must have been a few years older than her, between thirty-five and forty. He had short light brown hair, thick eyebrows, an angular face, stubble, and above all, those cold, calculating blue-gray eyes she found so fascinating. Alex felt she could have drowned in those irises. She knew she'd find no mercy in them, no remorse, and that excited her terribly.

He guided her into a large, soberly decorated living room. On the wall, she saw a degree in general medicine conferred to Matthieu Stan Grun. The man followed her gaze.

"Yes, that is my name. My friends call me Matt, but you will call me Master, understood?"

"Yes, Master."

"Good girl. Now undress yourself, lie down on this table with your legs spread wide, and close your eyes."

Alex obeyed, shivers of anticipation coursing through her body. She could hardly believe it was actually happening. She squirmed on the table, the anticipation as she heard Matt rummaging around for something killing her. She wanted to look, but she wasn't going to disobey now. Something was then jabbed into her neck and a cold liquid was injected into her. Despite her resolve, her eyes shot open in surprise.

"What was that?"

Matt slapped her hard.

"I told you to address me as Master. That, my dear whore, was a curare-based paralytic. You already feel yourself losing control of your body, don't you?"

Panic gripped Alex as her muscles progressively refused to obey her.

"Wait! That's not fair! That's not what we agreed on!"

Matt laughed darkly.

"Don't tell me you actually expected me to be nice to you. I warned you, didn't I? But don't worry, you won't be able to move, but you'll feel absolutely everything."

Alex sighed in relief and a satisfied smile spread across her face just before the paralysis took full effect. This time, Matt seemed slightly destabilized by her reaction, but he quickly recovered.

"You really are something else, aren't you? Let's give you what you came here for, then."

Matt grabbed a vibrating dildo and shoved it violently inside Alex's aching cunt. The paralysis made her extremely vulnerable to his assaults, ensuring that she couldn't move an inch to adjust to the insertion or make it less painful. This helplessness was exhilarating for her, increasing the pleasure the vibrations gave her tenfold. Matt pushed the dildo in as deep as he could, then pressed a Hitachi Magic Wand directly against her swollen clit. An intense orgasm racked her body, causing Matt to laugh and increase the intensity.

"Coming undone already? You sure are one eager little slut, but that was just the beginning."

He unzipped his pants, revealing a large, rock-hard, circumcised dick. He pressed it against Alex's anus and looked into her eyes.

"This is going to sting a bit." He grinned before brutally shoving it in. The penetration felt like scorching fire, but she still wanted more. More pleasure, more pain, more sensations, whatever they were. The curare continued to spread deeper and deeper into her system, causing her muscles to contract and making it difficult for her to breathe. She felt as if she had been reduced to nothing more than a giant cramp shaken by jolts of pleasure. A new orgasm hit her like a freight train while Matt was still going back and forth painfully inside her.

"It must be starting to really hurt now." Matt chuckled between pants. "Are you starting to have second thoughts? Do you want me to stop? Oh, that's right, you can't talk and I don't give a fuck anyway."

A third orgasm shook Alex, more painful than she'd thought possible. Her breathing was labored, and her muscle cramps were getting worse by the second. It was even better than in her wildest dreams. With a low grunt, Matt came deep inside her. He glanced at his watch.

"Right on time. The paralytic should be starting to wear off."

He grabbed a sharp scalpel and pushed it against Alex's throat, making a shallow cut. She felt her body slowly coming back under her control.

"Goodbye, sweetheart," the man mocked as his scalpel cut deeper into her throat excruciatingly slowly.

"Fuck yes! Kill me!" Alex uttered, her voice hoarse, as a new orgasm—more intense than the previous ones—shook her violently.

The man withdrew his scalpel and looked at Alex with a curious, amused expression.

"You're such an entertaining little thing. No, I think I'll keep you a little longer. It would be a waste to kill you right away," he said wonderingly, removing the vibrating toys.

"Thank you, Master," Alex breathed, her body still twitching, her dark eyes glazed over with pleasure.

"Now, like I said, you belong to me. Body and soul. I want you to give me all your private data. Your ID, your bank account, your social media passwords, everything. It all belongs to me now. Your life belongs to me, and I want to make sure you'll never be able to escape."

Alex complied, feeling a new wave of excitement sweep through her.

2. Cardigan

Alex woke up in Matt's basement, sore and weary. Her ass still hurt, and she was pretty sure something had ruptured, though she didn't mind. He had bandaged her throat before locking her in, promising he would procure the necessary items for their new arrangement the following day. Alex was eager to see what he meant. It was pitch-black in the basement, and she couldn't tell what time it was. Feeling her way around, she found a toilet and some locked cupboards. Not much to pass the time. She could only hope he'd be back soon to present her with new atrocities.

After what felt like hours, she heard footsteps growing nearer. The light was switched on from outside, and the door opened, revealing Matt's ominous figure, a bag in his hand. Alex leaped to her feet, her eyes sparkling with joy.

"So impatient to be humiliated." Matt laughed darkly. "How pathetic. Kneel, whore."

"Yes, Master." Alex knelt, feeling her pussy dripping wet.

He tossed black crotchless panties and a harness to her, which she slipped on immediately.

"Good girl," Matt sneered. This time, tossing her three vicious-looking alligator clamps linked together by a fine silver chain. "Now put those on."

Alex smiled as she recognized the item. She clipped the first clamp to her right nipple, gasping with delight as it bit down hard. Without hesitation, she applied the second clamp on her left nipple. She looked at the third one wonderingly, licking her lips in anticipation before she brushed it against her tender clit. The cold metal sent shivers through her sensitive flesh. With a loud moan, she let go at once, welcoming the sharp pain that followed as the device closed harshly. The chain was short and every movement pulled on it, inducing a pleasant tinge of pain.

"You'll be wearing this twenty-four seven unless told otherwise. I expect breakfast when I wake up and dinner when I get home from work.

The house must be kept clean at all times. Understood?"

"Yes, Master."

"Good girl. From now on, you'll sleep in the living room so that you can easily prepare my breakfast without me having to open the door, but you're forbidden to use any furniture. If you try to flee while you're home alone or call for help, all your personal data will be leaked. Believe me, you don't want that."

"I would never dream of running away," Alex answered truthfully.

"Now, I need to know: is someone going to be looking for you?"

Alex thought for a moment.

"My friends are used to me not contacting them for months at a time. If they're worried, all I have to do is send them a text saying everything's fine, and it won't be a problem. My boss, on the other hand, might not like me not coming to work."

Matt smiled with satisfaction and handed over her phone.

"You're going to call your work and tell them you're quitting. I'll let you know later if you need to reassure your friends."

Alex called her boss under Matt's watchful eye. He wasn't happy about her resigning without notice, but at least he wasn't going to send the police searching for her.

"Now that that's settled, I'll go and find a new victim since I'm not going to kill you right away after all. Do you think you can handle seeing me at work?"

"Yes, Master," she answered excitedly.

"There's a bottle of water and some food for you on the kitchen table. I calculated the quantities precisely. If you consume anything else, I'll know it and our deal will be off. No need to make me dinner today; I'll eat on the way."

Matt left the basement, leaving the door open and taking Alex's cell phone with him. Alex waited a few moments before leaving the room. Matt— Master—had asked her to keep the house clean, so that's what she was going to do. She'd never been a fan of domestic chores but with the clamps nagging at her aching parts and the promise of more horrors to come soon, the idea became way more interesting.

The curtains were drawn over all the windows, but she could see enough to know that the sun had already set. She'd probably spent most of the day in the basement, waiting for Master to return. Her throat was dry and her stomach rumbled vehemently when she remembered the food on the table. She entered the large modern kitchen and devoured the protein bar and water that Master had left for her. It didn't quell her hunger entirely, but she knew that while he wouldn't hesitate to famish her, he wouldn't let her starve to death. That wouldn't be a memorable ending.

Her meager meal over, Alex fetched the cleaning products and set to work. She was scouring the oven, bending over so that the clamps stung as much as possible, when she heard Master come in.

Alex hurried to greet him and saw that he was carrying an unconscious woman.

"Meet Carrington."

Alex watched the woman with interest. She was quite beautiful: plus-size, with long, straight black hair, nose and mouth piercings, tattoos, and wearing a black Star Wars T-shirt. Alex couldn't wait to find out what Master had in store for her.

"How do you know her name?" she asked curiously.

Master looked at her as if she was stupid.

"It was on her ID, whore. Found her at a train station; she must have been traveling around Europe by train, given all the tickets she was carrying. Looks like she's reached her last destination. Now go grab the red vibe from the cupboard, put it inside your pussy on low, and go kneel in the basement."

Alex obliged while Master dragged the woman—she couldn't remember her name, Cardigan, or something—to the basement. She found a little red vibrating egg in the drawer that

Master had pointed to, alongside many other sex toys. She went to the basement, where Master was busy tying up and undressing Cardigan. Alex knelt in front of them, her legs slightly spread, and inserted the egg set on low into her aching cunt. The vibration sent a warm wave of pleasure through her, but she knew that she'd need more to get herself to orgasm.

The woman was beginning to wake up. She opened her eyes and looked around in panic.

"Who are you? What do you want with me?"

"Do you like bugs, Carrington?" Master asked, ignoring her question and waving a key ring depicting several types of insects in front of her face.

Cardigan looked at him in silent horror.

"Since this was in your pocket, I'll take that as a yes," Master said. "I think I have just the thing for you. I've been saving them for the right occasion. I'll be back, don't move."

As he left the room, Cardigan's gaze fell on Alex.

Master put a second caterpillar on the speculum, then a third. Alex was still shifting her hips, breathing heavily as she imagined the agony Cardigan must be in. The woman was still screaming, her face red and her eyes full of tears. Master grabbed a scalpel and ran it teasingly over Cardigan's body, then, without warning, cut off her right nipple.

Alex gasped. Suddenly, she didn't know whether she wanted to be in Cardigan's place, or in Master's. The rush she got from seeing someone else suffer was almost as good as the one she got from her own suffering, and she knew it would be even more thrilling if she were the one holding the scalpel.

Master tossed the severed nipple at her, pushing her out of her reverie.

"Eat it, whore. And don't use your hands."

Alex, who had always been curious about the taste of human flesh, leaned forward, savoring the pinch of the clamps. She took the piece of flesh from the dirty floor between her teeth and chewed slowly, letting it flood her taste buds. The first taste that came to her was that of coppery blood, then a second layer revealed itself, similar to that of pork, only sweeter.

By the time Alex was done chewing, Master was cutting off Cardigan's arm—which was decorated with a cute little lantern tattoo—with what she assumed must be a medical bone saw. The woman was crying and screaming her lungs out.

Alex wondered if Master would ever cut one of her own arms off. She had to admit, she was a little bit jealous, but hey, if she wanted to try and torture someone herself, it would be good to have both arms.

A finger removed, then, maybe? Just to try it?

Master finished severing Cardigan's arm with a sickening sound of cracking bone and tearing flesh. She had gone deathly pale, and her howls had reverted to weak whimpers. Master made her lie on her stomach and covered her mangled arm with the blood that flowed abundantly from her stump.

He took a second speculum and used it to widen Cardigan's asshole, then pushed her own hand inside it, eliciting a gasp from the woman. Master kept pushing the arm in, and Alex watched in fascination as the limb sank deeper and deeper into its owner. Its progress seemed to become more cumbersome when it reached the elbow, but Master kept pushing, and the joint eventually disappeared too.

"Come and suck me off, whore," he barked at Alex.

He sounded very different from the calm and collected demeanor he usually showed, the bloodlust no doubt bringing out a more animalistic side of him. Still on her knees, she crawled up to him, undid his fly, and took his large shaft in her mouth. Master grabbed Alex's hair with one hand and forced his cock all the way down her throat, blocking her airway, his other hand pushing the arm into Cardigan's asshole. Alex loved the feeling of his dick hitting the back of her throat with bruising force while she was struggling for air, but the low vibe denying her any release was the real torture.

From the corner of her eyes, she saw blood pouring from Cardigan's mouth as the arm nearly disappeared inside her. With a low grunt, Master came in Alex's mouth; it was a salty taste that mixed wonderfully with the lingering one of Cardigan's left nipple.

"Clean this mess, whore," Master ordered, pushing her away with enough force to make her fall to her side.

She looked at Cardigan's mangled form; blood was still trickling from her mouth, but she had stopped breathing. A low laugh escaped Alex's throat when she noted that the arm sticking out of the woman's asshole looked like a grotesque, pathetic tail. She didn't mind cleaning everything up, but she hoped she would at least get a reward.

"What about me?" she moaned, moving her hips up and down.

Master pulled the vibe out of her and sneered.

"You? What made you think that you would

get anything? Now I want you to put the body in one of those bags,"—he pointed at a pile of large plastic bags—"drag it to my car, then clean the blood from the floor while I'm disposing of the body."

Master left the basement without another word, leaving Alex horny and disappointed. She wasn't sure she liked the way things were going; all she wanted was to experience intense sensations, and having them denied wasn't something she was interested in or enjoyed in the slightest. She sighed. He'd promiscd her a memorable death, and she'd seen what he was capable of. It was well worth the sacrifice, and in the meantime, she could always take care of herself.

She pulled Cardigan's severed arm slightly out of her hole and crouched over it, forcing it into her swollen cunt. She was so turned on she felt her orgasm grow near after only a couple of bounces. She gasped, closing her eyes. It was release, sure, and it was good, but nowhere as intense as what she wanted. She suspected it would have been much more interesting if Cardigan had still been alive and suffering.

With a disappointed sigh, she put the body into one of the bags, as Master had instructed, and dragged it out of the house. She had to pause several times to catch her breath and rest her muscles, but she didn't give up. Exhausted and sweating, she finally set the body bag down beside Master's car when a shuffling noise caught her attention. She turned to see a possum looking at her with a curious expression. Alex returned the puzzled glance. She'd never seen a possum in the wild and wasn't even sure there were supposed to be any in Switzerland. Maybe this one had escaped from a zoo.

"Hey there, girl," she called, "come here!"

The possum made no sign of approaching, so Alex tore a small piece of flesh from Cardigan's corpse and placed it in the palm of her outstretched hand. This time, the possum came closer cautiously, grabbed the piece of flesh, and after sniffing it suspiciously, devoured it happily and even let Alex pet her.

"I like you, girl." Alex laughed. "Human flesh does taste good, doesn't it? I should give you a name. What about Garbage? It's a nice name for a possum, right?"

Garbage squealed happily and scurried away. Alex went back inside to clean the blood off the floor while Master disposed of the body. The tugging of the clamps as she worked, kneeling against the cold, hard basement floor, soon made her almost as desperate again as she had been before she fucked herself with Cardigan's arm. She finished cleaning the basement and moved on to cleaning the rest of the house once more. She was scrubbing the bathroom floor when she heard the door open and two men walk in. She recognized Master's voice but had no idea who the second man was. The uncertainty alone made her dripping wet, and she hurried off to greet them.

The second man was tall, in his twenties, red-haired, with piercing brown eyes and freckles. He looked her up and down, smiling hungrily.

"So that's your pet whore? She does look pretty for a slut. I'm Elias Montgomery, but you will call me Sir."

"Yes, Sir," Alex replied, grinding her hips together in anticipation.

"You trained her well." Elias nodded approvingly to Master.

"Trained her?" Master chuckled, looking at her with contempt. "She was already a desperate whore when I found her, begging for my cock and my knife."

"Well then, let us give her both. It would be cruel of us to deny her."

Alex's stomach filled with butterflies. Finally! It was her turn! Part of her hoped they wouldn't kill her so she could experiment with torturing someone else, but the other part didn't give a fuck what happened as long as it felt good.

"Go lie in the basement, on your stomach, with your legs open like the little bitch in heat you are," Master commanded.

Alex nearly ran down the stairs. Her breathing

heavy with lust and anticipation, she lay on her stomach, spreading her legs as wide as she could. Master and his friend arrived sometime after, walking excruciatingly slowly. She couldn't see them in the position she was in, but she could hear their footsteps. When something cold and sharp pressed against her cunt, she tried to turn around to get a better view, but Elias appeared in front of her and held her firmly in place.

"Don't move, whore, or you could get seriously hurt," he snarled.

"You don't want the fun to stop so soon, now, do you?" Master added. "Here's what's going to happen. I'm going to put this knife inside your filthy cunt and it's going to stay there while we fuck you. If you stand very still, you should manage with a few scratches, maybe a couple of small cuts. Nothing that will stop you from feeling. But if you move, well, it could be really bad. You might not die, but you'd lose all sensation. No more orgasms for you. Understood?"

"Yes, Master."

Alex shuddered at the thought. It was both terrifying and exhilarating. The blade slid inside her, making her gasp. She could feel it scratching her, but like Master had promised, it didn't seem like it would do more as long as she stood perfectly still.

Master forced his cock inside her ass. It burned, and it was all she could do not to shift her hips. Elias grabbed her hair and pulled her face close to his crotch.

"Will you suck it like a good bitch?"

"Yes, Sir," she breathed.

"Good."

He shoved his dick down her throat. Both men fucked her mercilessly, overwhelming her with pain and pleasure. The sensation was so good that she couldn't help but buck her hips, causing the knife to bite lightly into her vaginal wall. She stopped moving immediately, her eyes widening as the men laughed at her. Elias pushed his shaft all the way down Alex's throat and held it there, pressing her nose against his firm stomach. She found herself gasping for air while trying to remain as still as possible. Soon, her brain switched into alarm mode and panic kicked in, causing her to jerk violently. The blade bit deeper, adding a second layer of panic to the physiological reaction. What if she damaged a nerve and lost all sensation like Master had said? That would be too horrible. She couldn't even think about it. She tried to force her body to remain still, but it wouldn't listen, and the knife bit her once more. Elias came down her throat and finally released her, laughing as she struggled to regain her breath. Master came not long after. He removed the knife and examined her cunt.

"You got lucky," he said, sounding almost disappointed. "That last one got you pretty deep but failed to inflict any substantial damage. It will heal soon enough. Now go clean yourself up, you look filthy."

When Alex got out of the shower and back into the living room, Master and Sir Elias were talking and laughing together, not paying any attention to her.

"My cousin Isaac would have loved this," Elias was saying. "Did I ever tell you about his first time? He was supposed to kill a dumb cat with a bunch of his friends, but one of the kids chickened out and let it get away, so they beat him up instead. A couple of weeks later, the girls in the group held that kid down while Isaac and another dude cut and fucked him to make sure he'd really learned his lesson. Too bad he still lives in the US, or I would have invited him next time."

Next time. The words filled Alex with glee. Later that night, when she went to sleep on the living room floor, naked and clamped, she played the scene over and over in her head until she fell asleep, smiling.

3. Toy

"Master?" Alex asked tentatively. She was kneeling on the floor eating her meager breakfast, while Master sat at the table eating the pancakes and drinking the coffee she made for him. "Could I torture the next one with you? Please?"

Master looked at her with disdain and she was sure he was going to say no, but then a wicked grin spread across his face.

"Sure, whore. Now go put yourself away in that cupboard. The house is clean enough for the moment, and I would prefer it if you don't run around while I'm at work."

"But, Master? What about your dinner?"

Master took a timer padlock out of his pocket.

"I will use this device to lock you in. It will open exactly one hour before I come home. I expect everything to be ready by then."

Alex wasn't thrilled by the prospect of spending hours doing absolutely nothing, but she obliged and let Master close the door. She made herself as comfortable as possible in the cramped space that only allowed her to crouch down, and she waited for the time to pass.

If only Master had stuffed her full of high-speed vibes, forcing her to come over and over for hours on end with no hope of escape, each time more painful than the last, now that would have been fun. This isolation was torture, and not in a fun way. She was bored out of her mind, and even the clamps didn't do much to stimulate her anymore. She had grown used to the pain, and it was no more than a pleasant tingle. After a while, her muscles started to ache, and she found herself hoping that the pain would soon become unbearable, but it never rose above a dull soreness.

When the padlock finally opened with a loud *click*, Alex sighed with relief and hurried out of the cupboard. Cooking Master's meal wasn't something she particularly enjoyed, but at least it was *something*. The monotonous normality of the everyday life she was used to instead of absolute nothingness.

4

Alex watched Master eat his dinner, waiting for him to acknowledge her. He tossed some mashed potato to the ground and observed her as she licked it up.

"I took a couple of weeks off from work. I haven't taken any vacations in a while, and I want to concentrate on my hobby. What about you, whore? How was your day?" he asked, a hint of malice in his calm tone.

"It was horrible," Alex answered truthfully. "I thought I was going to die of boredom."

"That's good to know." He chuckled darkly. "You'll be locked in the cupboard again tomorrow, then my vacation will start and we'll go on a hunt together. You'll be a good whore and do as I say even if you don't like it."

"Yes, Master," she answered, feeling her chest tighten. "Could I at least have something to pass the time, please? Forced orgasms? Electric shocks? Pins on the ground? Some kind of drug? Anything? Please?"

"I love it when you beg to be abused. There are so many ways I could hurt you, but for now, I'll have to deny your wish."

Master retreated to his room without so much as touching her. Alex took care of the dishes and curled up on the ground, fighting back tears. She knew that enduring the cupboard again would be worth it, that Master would not disappoint her, but it was so frustrating.

The next day, when Master locked the cupboard door again, Alex found herself wishing that she was claustrophobic or, at least, afraid of the dark. With a deep, shaky sigh, she closed her eyes. Maybe the house would catch fire and she would remain trapped in here, unable to escape as the cruel flames licked her legs, her stomach, her chest, enveloping her in a coat of unfathomable agony before finally taking her away with them. Or maybe there would be a flood. A really big one that miraculously managed to engulf the whole cupboard.

Wishful thinking. It would get her nowhere, but then again, neither would anything else. She started fingering herself as she imagined the water slowly filling up the cupboard. She would struggle, trying to smash the door with her feet, but nothing would work. Maybe she'd break her foot or knee in the process? The water would keep rising until only her head remained. By that point, she would then know that nothing could save her.

Her fingers moved faster inside herself, a wonderful warmth enveloping her. The water would continue to rise mercilessly, submerging her mouth, then finally her nose. She would hold her breath as long as possible, but the pressure would eventually become too much. She'd reflexively take a deep breath, the water rushing into her lungs, burning her. She would panic, feeling life leave her, her frantic lungs desperately trying to inhale air but finding only water.

She climaxed hard as she imagined her lifeless body floating limply in the flooded closet.

The rest of the day passed in a blur. She clung to Master's promise to find someone for them to torture together so as not to sink into despair. When she finally heard the *click* of the lock, she all but ran to the kitchen to prepare dinner.

Once again, Master came home and ate his dinner without paying any attention to Alex.

"Clean this and get dressed," he ordered once finished.

Alex put on the clothes she had arrived in over her clamps. This made her sufficiently presentable not to be arrested for indecency, but it wouldn't be hard for anyone to guess what the small chain disappearing under her top and skirt really was.

Master put her in his car and drove off into the night.

"You stay close to me and do exactly what I tell you, and in a few hours, at most, we will have a new friend to play with."

Master stopped the car in a dark alley near a busy bar-lined street close to Plainpalais. After many long minutes of waiting, a man walked by. He looked to be some twink in his early to mid-twenties, punk style, long and wavy light brown hair, some piercings, eyeliner, a dark red T-shirt, a tie covered in safety pins, ripped jeans, and shiny black Doc Martens. Judging by his uncertain gait and reddened eyes, he was tipsy and possibly high.

"This one will be an easy target," Master said. "Go and distract him for me, whore."

"With pleasure, Master. I bet he's a slut. Maybe not in practice but in his mind, that's for sure. He's going to love this."

Master smiled at her, looking genuinely amused. It was the first time he looked at her like that, and it made her heart flutter. She got out of the car and walked up to the man.

"Hey there, pretty boy!" She gave him her brightest smile. "You look as bored as I am. Maybe we could keep each other company?"

The man looked her up and down, his eyes unfocused.

"I'm not paying."

"I'm not a whore." Alex laughed. "I mean, I am, but not the kind that you need to pay. I'm Alex, by the way."

"Julien," the man answered.

"Well then, Julien," Alex whispered into his ear, throwing her arms around his neck, "what do you say we have some fun?"

Master chose this moment to come out of the shadows and press a damp cloth against Julien's nose. They both held him still as he struggled, one hand over his mouth to stop him from calling for help, until he lost consciousness and collapsed.

"Didn't look like much of a slut to me." Master laughed.

"I guess he's too shy to admit it yet." Alex grinned. "But you'll see."

Alex waited with Master for Julien to wake up. They had undressed him and put him in the basement, but they didn't tie him up, as Master wanted to test Alex's theory. When the man finally opened his eyes, he seemed to have sobered up a little. He looked at them in confusion before noticing his surroundings and his nakedness. He crawled back against the wall in a panic, covering himself up with his hands.

"Have you ever been fucked in the ass before, boy?" Master asked, his crude words contrasting with his formal demeanor.

His eyes wide with fear, Julien shook his head no. Master looked at Alex as if to say what he was thinking, I *knew* it. Alex smiled slyly. She was still certain she was right, and this little test was about to prove it.

"I'll be back in exactly thirty minutes to fuck you," Master informed Julien. "I advise you to make yourself ready, or it could be very painful for you."

Julien looked in horror at the collection of toys and the tube of lube standing near him in the basement. Master and Alex left the room, locking him in, and Master guided Alex to a room she'd never been allowed in before, where a screen showed what was happening in the basement.

"There's a camera in there?" Alex asked, surprised.

"Of course there is. Oh, by the way, I never asked, Did you have fun with Carrington's arm?"

"Not as much as I'd hoped," she confessed.

Master seemed satisfied with that answer, and they both returned their attention to the screen. Julien was staring at the toys, the conflict evident on his face. He carefully picked up the smallest plug, ran his hand through his hair with uncertainty, then opened the lube bottle and poured a generous amount on the plug. Swallowing hard, he slowly pushed it between his legs. Alex let out a triumphant exclamation, pumping her fist.

"People will do anything out of fear," Master grunted. "Doesn't prove anything."

Julien shifted the plug around for a while, then moved it back and forth, slowly at first, before picking up speed. Tears were running down his cheeks, but his cock was getting hard. Alex looked smugly at Master. He grabbed her by the throat and squeezed.

"You may have been right on this one, but don't get too cocky," he snarled, a glint of amusement in his eyes.

"Sorry, Master," Alex gasped, loving every second of it.

Julien replaced the small plug with a bigger one and repeated the operation. By the end of the thirty minutes, he was vigorously fucking himself with a fairly large dildo, sobbing, and sporting a raging boner.

"I think I'm going to keep this one for a while," Master informed Alex. "You can watch while I fuck him, then we'll leave him alone with his thoughts for a while. Don't worry, you'll still get to torture him later."

Julien gasped and let the dildo fall to the ground as soon as they opened the door. His cheeks turned bright red, and he looked down in shame. Master pushed him onto his stomach, pressing his face against the cold hard floor, and shoved his cock roughly in his gaping hole. Alex focused on the younger man's face. It was contorted, his eyes squeezed shut while a mixture of wails and moans escaped from his half-open mouth. She couldn't help but touch herself, imagining she was in his place. The way fear, shame, humiliation, and arousal were certainly mingling inside him must have been truly exquisite.

Master came with a grunt deep inside the boy, and Alex immediately followed suit. Julien curled up into a shaking ball, revealing a stain of cum where his dick had been pressed against the concrete floor. Alex smiled smugly at Master as he pushed Julien's head against it.

"Lick it clean, you disgusting cumrag."

Julien took a deep breath before obliging. His pink tongue explored the ground tentatively, his face twisting in revulsion. Despite his obvious disgust, he cleaned the entire spill, swallowing uneasily. Once he was done, Alex and Master left the room, locking him in the dark.

"Fine, maybe you were right," Master admitted. "I imagine it takes a slut to know another, hmm? Now go clean the bathroom. I'll call you when it's time to pay our new friend a little visit."

Alex walked to the bathroom with a shit-eating grin. She loved being right. The bathroom was already mostly clean, so she set to work to make it entirely spotless. A couple of hours later, the gray glazed tile floor was shiny, and the bathtub and toilet looked as if they had just come from the store. Right on cue, as Master called her just seconds after she'd finished. She went down to join him and saw he was holding a bowl of dog food in his hand.

"A suitable food for a filthy little bitch, don't you think?"

"Absolutely, Master."

When they opened the basement door, Julien gasped and cowered against the wall. Master put the bowl down in front of him.

"Eat it, bitch. Tomorrow will be a long, painful day for you. But who knows? Maybe you'll enjoy it."

They left the room again, this time leaving the light on, and went back to the observation room.

"Do you think he'll actually eat it?" Alex asked.

"He sobered up partly, but he's still high. Did you not see his eyes? He will be craving food. Add to that his fear and the fact that he's not in full possession of his mental faculties at the moment, and of course, he is going to eat it."

Indeed, Julien took a small bite, then another, bigger one.

"I can't believe it!" Master laughed. "Look at this! He's getting hard again!"

"I guess he has a thing for humiliation. Or maybe it was your threat that got him."

"Maybe both. But to be fair, the drugs in his system must have something to do with it too. Cannabis is known to increase sex drive and arousal."

Looking dreadfully ashamed, Julien grabbed a medium-sized dildo and pushed it inside himself. He kept eating the dog food while fucking himself with the toy and moaning. Alex had to admit, she was impressed. Sure, the weed undoubtedly had something to do with it, but that guy was more of a slut than she had expected. If he just needed to take care of his boner, nothing was stopping him from simply using his hand. She couldn't wait to hurt him.

He came as he finished his bowl, shooting thick ropes of seed onto the floor, then dropped the dildo, looking horrified by what he had just done.

"Go wait for me outside the basement," Master ordered. "I just got an idea and I need to grab something."

Alex settled herself right next to the basement door, enjoying the pathetic muffled whimpers she heard on the other side. Master soon joined her, a wireless tattoo gun in hand. He entered the basement and strode towards Julien, who backed away in panic.

"Since you'll be here for a while, I think you should have a name."

"It's Jul—" Julien started, but Master kicked him hard in the crotch, causing him to double over.

"You don't deserve a human name, you pathetic cumrag. You're nothing more than a filthy little fucktoy, so from now on, you will be named toy. You'll call me Master, and you can call the whore Miss. Understood?"

Toy nodded slowly.

"Good. Whore, please hold it still. I want to make sure it remembers its place."

Alex really liked the idea; it was beautifully demeaning. She had no trouble keeping him still as she was more muscular than he was, and he was too exhausted or shocked to put up much of a fight anyway. *Or maybe he wanted it to happen,* she thought with a smile.

Master tattooed the word *toy* on his forehead while he wept quietly. Master added the word *cumrag* in large letters across toy's chest, then held a pocket mirror in front of him so he could admire the result. Toy curled up, sobbing. A truly magnificent vision.

Once they'd climbed back up, Alex saw something moving outside the living room window. She looked more closely and noticed a possum watching her from the garden.

"Garbage!" she exclaimed, laughing.

"What?" Master groaned.

"That possum out there." She pointed. "I already saw her when I took out that girl's body. I

47

named her Garbage. I gave her a piece of flesh and she loved it. Maybe she knows that we have another victim and is hoping for more food?"

"An anthropophagous possum in our garden? That's a new one." Master chuckled. "Well, let's give her what she wants, I'd hate to disappoint her. Just hold still."

Alex bit her lip in anticipation as Master pulled out his scalpel. Delicately, almost sensuously, he cut a small piece of flesh from the top of Alex's thigh. The burn of the blade inflamed her crotch, making her crave more, but it ended all too soon. Master was done for now.

She followed him into the garden and giggled when Garbage, after looking at her as if waiting for her confirmation that it was safe, rushed over and greedily swallowed the chunk of her thigh. The possum let them both pet her belly, making satisfied squeaks before heading off into the bushes again.

4. Fucking Her Brains Out

The next day, Master took Alex out in search of a new victim, explaining that he wanted to make the most of his time off, that no one would notice toy's disappearance, and that the cops were too stupid to catch him anyway. Not that Alex had any complaints. She loved their little game with toy, but she was excited to finally properly torture someone.

They set up in an alleyway in the industrial zone of Vernier. Master remained discreetly in his car parked a little ways away while Alex waited outside, ready to act as bait. She was dressed in the same way as the previous day, with the addition of a bandage where Master had cut off a piece of her thigh to feed Garbage. If she came across a straight-looking man or a queer-looking woman—or whoever else might be attracted to women, for that matter—she was sure she'd be able to seduce them or, at least, intrigue them enough to give Master time to act. Otherwise, she'd play the poor lost girl in need of help.

A cute black-haired girl with piercings and tattoos came down the street. Alex decided there was a good chance she wasn't straight.

"Hi there, beautiful!" Alex began, smiling seductively. "I think I got a bit lost here. I'm looking for Meyrin. You wouldn't happen to know the way, would you?"

"I'm not from around here, sorry," the woman answered in an American accent. Southern, maybe? Alex wasn't sure. But what was important was that, by the way her eyes were roaming over Alex's body, she knew she'd been right.

"Oh, well, no worries. I'll find it eventually. By the way, I love your shirt." Alex bit her lips playfully, letting her eyes trail on the woman's purple shirt.

"Thank you, I love yours too," she answered, blushing and visibly flustered. "I'm Lyndie, by the way. Lyndie Lei."

Before Alex could reply, Master arrived with a damp cloth and pressed it to Lyndie's nose, just as he had done to toy sometime earlier.

ᖙ

Master decided to play with Lyndie in the bathroom rather than the basement to avoid interfering with his plans for toy. He handed Alex a small, sharp knife.

"Go on, show me what you can do."

Alex beamed with glee. Finally, it was her turn to have fun! She looked at Lyndie's bound, gagged figure. The woman had just woken up and was glancing around desperately.

Alex thought for a moment, observing the knife intently before making up her mind. She grabbed Lyndie's hand and dug the knife under one of her fingernails, using it as leverage to pull it off. The woman screamed through her gag; the muffled sound caused a pleasurable tingle in Alex's crotch. Before she could get to work on the second nail, the sound of scratching at the door startled her. Master hurried to open it, armed with his scalpel, and Garbage slipped between his legs to run to Alex.

"How did you get in?" Alex laughed, scratching the animal's belly.

"Probably one of the cracked windows." Master chuckled. "She really is something else, your little anthropophagic possum."

Garbage squealed with delight and sniffed at the torn nail.

"You can't eat that, baby." Alex laughed. "Wait, I'll give you something better."

She cut a large strip of flesh from Lyndie's leg and gave it to Garbage, who ate it happily, painting her little furry mouth and nose red with blood.

Lyndie looked as if she'd seen a ghost, her face a mask of terror and confusion. Alex dug her blade under her fingernail a second time, moaning slightly as she peeled it off. Master grunted in approval and pushed her away.

"My turn, now."

Alex was about to protest, outraged that he stopped her so soon when she'd barely begun to enjoy herself, but she held her tongue when she saw him pull out his cock and place it in front of Lyndie's right eye. This was intriguing enough for her not to complain, at least for now.

Master held the woman's head steady and pushed his dick into her eye. Lyndie squeezed it shut, but the thin membrane of her eyelids was far from offering sufficient shielding, and her eyeball burst with a *splosh* under the force of the assault. A couple more brutal thrusts, and her sphenoid bone broke with a sickening *crunch*. Chunks of bone, eyeball, and gray matter ran down Lyndie's cheek like nightmarish tears as Master continued to fuck her brains out, burying his shaft up to his balls in the emptying eye socket.

"She's so lucky." Alex sighed.

"You really think she likes that?" Master panted. "You are delusional, do you know that?"

"If I did, I wouldn't be delusional, now, would I?"

"That's . . . not exactly how it works, but you have a point," Master groaned between thrusts.

Lyndie's wails and horrified flails continued

for a brief moment before she went limp. Master tossed her dead body aside and buried himself inside Alex instead, holding her against the wall by the throat. She gasped in pleasure as the fluid-coated dick penetrated her, her bliss magnified tenfold by the sight of Lyndie's mutilated face, her optic nerve dangling flaccidly, still attached to the back of a smashed eyeball. Master came with a grunt and pushed her aside like he had just done with Lyndie's body.

"Hey! I wasn't finished!" Alex complained.

"Bitches like you don't deserve to finish," Master sneered. "And don't you dare touch yourself without my permission."

Alex sighed. She really didn't like the way this was going, but it'd be worth it in the end. Garbage was happily eating the corpse, uninterested in what the two humans next to her were doing. Alex smiled at her. She was so carefree, so cheerful, with her little furry face covered in blood, brains, and ocular fluid. So precious.

"Come on, whore. Let's go play with toy; I'm

not done having fun. You'll clean this mess later," Master ordered.

"Take your time, girl," Alex told Garbage. "You can join us when you're done."

Master chuckled, but he didn't make any comment as Alex followed him toward the basement. Toy flinched as they entered, then curled up against the far wall, looking at them pleadingly.

"I didn't give you time to prepare this time, sorry," Master mocked. "Kneel with your legs apart and your arms behind your back. Now."

Toy submitted meekly, and Alex grinned as she saw the beginning of an erection forming between his legs. She playfully traced the healing *cumrag* tattoo on his chest with her fingers, causing him to shiver. Master walked behind him, grabbed his wrist with one hand, his hair with the other, and forced himself balls-deep inside him in one powerful thrust. Toy trembled at the violent intrusion, his eyes rolling back in agony while his legs shook uncontrollably.

Alex's arousal only grew stronger at the sight of his pain and fear. She grabbed his balls and twisted them roughly, delighting in his screams. Despite the misery he was in, toy's shaft was now fully erect. Alex punched him in the stomach and genitals, moaning in harmony with his cries. Toy tried to protect himself or double over in pain, but Master was holding him firmly in place, fucking him tirelessly.

Alex had never had so much fun in her life. She just wished she would be allowed to use him to pleasure herself. She grabbed his cock in one hand and his balls in the other and yanked sharply, spreading them apart and making him howl in pure suffering. Master came a second time and as usual, tossed his used plaything to the side, taking only the minutest interest in it now that he'd got what he wanted. Alex looked at him hopefully, but he made no sign of wanting to touch her.

"Can I pleasure myself now, please, Master?" she finally asked.

"You really are a greedy slut, aren't you? No.

You cannot pleasure yourself."

She gritted her teeth and accepted the challenge. She knew that he would satisfy her eventually and that it would be all she'd ever wished for and more. She just had to hold on a little bit longer.

Toy was struggling to catch his breath, his frail body convulsing, curled up on the ground and racked with sobs.

"This must be the happiest day of his life," Alex whispered wonderingly.

"This is starting to bug me," Master replied, frowning. "Do you really, honestly believe that they enjoy this? I mean, sure, he got hard, but that's just a physiological reflex. Look at him, does he seem to be happy? And that bitch, Lyndie? How on earth can you think that she enjoyed getting her eyeball fucked into her skull?"

"Didn't you hear the way they moaned? The thrill, the exquisite pain, it's the most beautiful thing in the world."

"The most— I'm sorry, have you ever heard

stories from serial killer survivors? They didn't enjoy the experience, they got fucking traumatized! I can't believe I'm the one telling you this. God, if I didn't plan on killing you once I'm done playing with you, I'd tell you to go get therapy."

Alex shrugged. Master didn't understand, but it didn't matter. As long as she got what she wanted in the end, he could believe whatever the hell he wanted.

"Anyway," Master smirked sadistically, changing the subject, "I have a little surprise for you both. You're going to hate this."

Alex followed him back to the living room, delicious anxiety gnawing at her stomach. Master theatrically pulled two chastity devices out of a drawer, one male and one female.

"Put this on," he ordered, tossing the female one at Alex. "That way, I won't have to worry about you finishing yourself off behind my back."

Alex looked at the chastity belt in horror.

"Wait, no, please. That's not funny."

"Remember our deal? You belong to me, body and soul. Or maybe you'd prefer I kill you right now? I have a nice poison that will make your death entirely painless. It will be like falling asleep. You won't feel a thing."

"No!" Alex screamed. "I'll put it on, I'll put it on! Just . . . don't give me a painless death. Please. Anything but that. I want to feel everything."

"Good girl. Go ahead, then. Put it on."

Alex tugged at her clit clamp hesitantly, looking at Master for instruction. It felt like a bad idea to put the chastity belt over it, but he hadn't explicitly told her to remove it either.

Master nodded. "Take it off. The ones on your nipples too. You barely feel them anymore anyway, do you?"

Alex did as she was told. Master was right; she had grown numb to the pain, so she didn't mind removing them. The blood rushing back to her sensitive parts sent a pleasant, painful shiver through her nipples and clit, but it was short-lived as the clamps hadn't been tight enough to really cut off circulation. The metal belt felt cold against her privates, and she shivered when Master locked it in place.

"Now let's give toy his present," Master sneered, grabbing a big paper bag.

They went back to the basement. Toy was still sobbing, curled up on the cold hard floor, and barely looked up when they came back in. Master fastened the small male chastity cage around his limp cock while he whined pitifully, then revealed the contents of the bag: a shock collar attached to a leash, a black leather chest harness, a similar leg harness, and finally a face harness with an O-ring gag attached.

Master fastened all the gear on an unmoving, whimpering toy.

"If we keep you around for a while, we might as well make you useful. My whore will show you what to do. Oh, and you only crawl on all fours from now on, obviously." He handed the leash to Alex. "Now go clean the bathroom, both of you."

Alex took toy's leash and yanked it until he

started crawling behind her. She loved the feeling of power that it gave her. He followed her to the bathroom, looking even more frightened than before, if that was even possible. He stopped dead in his tracks when he saw Lyndie's corpse and tried to run away, but Alex was stronger than him and held his leash firmly. She pressed the trigger to his shock collar for good measure, grinding her hips together as he collapsed and writhed in pain.

"Oh no, you're not going anywhere, cumrag. This bathroom needs to be spotless, and it's your problem now. Go ahead, put the body in the bag." She turned to Garbage who was snoring softly, curled up next to the body. "Did you enjoy your meal, girl? We have to clear the table now but don't worry, there'll be more."

Toy tentatively grabbed the corpse to put it in the bag, but no sooner had he touched it than he recoiled as if he'd received another electric shock, hurrying to vomit into the bathtub.

"Seriously?" Alex sighed, grabbing him by his long hair and slapping him hard. "You're a sensitive little bitch, you know that? Now put that fucking body in the fucking bag before I get fucking angry."

Drool and vomit dripping from his ring gag, toy complied. He was ashen but managed to do as he was told without retching a second time.

"See, it wasn't that hard, was it? Now clean this mess." Alex handed him a sponge and cleaning products. She smiled wickedly, enjoying the sight of toy on all fours cleaning the blood and vomit. She'd scrubbed this bathroom so many times in the last few days, it was nice to pass the task on to someone else.

"Get into the tub, your turn to get cleaned up now" she ordered once he was done.

She cleaned the puke and gore off of him, then positioned the showerhead right over his mouth and nose, holding his wrist tightly so he couldn't defend himself. She laughed, watching him squirm and struggle to catch his breath. She quickly released him, not wanting to accidentally drown him, and smirked sadistically as he coughed water.

Master raised an amused eyebrow when she

walked back into the living room, pulling behind her a toy that looked like a drowned dog, but he didn't comment. He took the leash from her and let her drag the body bag to the car. Garbage lazily opened her eyes and followed her outside, where she disappeared into the bushes again. When Alex walked back into the house, Master had their dinners ready: a cereal bar for her and a bowl of dog food on the floor for toy. He poured the contents of a little vial into the bowl and unfastened the ring gag. Toy eyed the food dubiously.

"I'm sorry, does it look like I'm giving you a choice?" Master mocked. "If you really must know, it was a potent aphrodisiac of my making in the vial. Now eat."

He pushed toy's face into the bowl, leaving him no option but to comply if he wanted to breathe.

5. Russian Roulette

It had been three days already since Master put Alex in chastity. Three long, harrowing days of pure torture, and not in a fun way.

She was kneeling on the floor next to toy, whose leash was attached to the table leg, while Master ate the meal they had prepared together for him. She had to admit, using him as a slave and pushing him around was fun. If only she wasn't caged . . .

"I'm going to hire a prostitute tonight," Master informed them casually.

"Are we going to kill her?" Alex asked, her heart fluttering with excitement at the prospect.

"Kill her? No, I'm going to make her orgasm over and over again while you watch."

"That's unfair! When will I be able to come?"

"The more you complain, the less I want to pleasure you, you know?" Master chuckled.

Alex held back a snarky reply, annoyed. She glanced at toy; the poor thing was in a much worse state than she was. A steady trickle of drool flowed from his ring gag, and his battered cock—feverish from the copious amounts of aphrodisiac Master made him swallow every day—was pressing helplessly against his tight cage. He couldn't help but tug at the device and grind pathetically against every hard surface he could find, offering his ass up and hoping to be fucked every time Master looked his way. Sure, Alex wasn't a fan of being kept in chastity, but she could convince herself that it was kind of fun, in a way, if she really thought about it. Toy, on the other hand, seemed to be in utter misery. This was one of the hottest things she'd ever seen.

⛧

The sex worker arrived later that night. She was a gorgeous ginger dressed in black leather who called herself Cinnabar. Toy had been locked in the basement to be on the safe side. Although they hadn't seen any *Missing Person* posters for him, and the aphrodisiac messed with his mind too much for him to even think about calling for help, Master didn't want to take any chances.

"Are you ready?" Master asked Cinnabar.

"I'm always ready." Cinnabar grinned. "You said you wanted to tie me up and force orgasms on me while your sub watches, right? How do you want to do this?"

"Just take off your clothes and sit on that chair. I'll take care of the rest. Oh, and let me know if it is getting to be too much."

"Don't worry about it, babe. Forced orgasms are one of my specialties. I could go on all night long!"

Cinnabar removed her clothes sensually, revealing smooth skin and cute, perky breasts. She sat on the chair and let Master tie her up securely with black rope. Once he was satisfied that she wouldn't be able to move an inch, he pressed the Hitachi Magic Wand right against her clit, and secured it in place so she wouldn't be able to escape the vibrations.

"Kneel in front of her and don't you dare look away," he ordered Alex before turning on the wand.

Cinnabar gasped in delight. Alex watched enviously as the sex worker's breathing grew deeper, her breasts rising and falling faster and faster as moans of pleasure escaped her lips. Alex couldn't help but grind her legs against each other, desperate for any friction she might get. Cinnabar came with a scream, squirting over the wand. She closed her eyes, squirming on the chair, unable to move the object a single inch.

Alex swallowed hard. God, she needed to feel something, anything. Pain, pleasure, anything but that nothingness Master seemed to enjoy inflicting on her. Cinnabar came again, her whole body trembling. Master increased the intensity of the vibrations. Cinnabar was racked by tremors, her body shining with a thin layer of sweat as she moaned and screamed in delight.

Alex lost track of how many times the woman had come by the time Master released her.

Cinnabar took a few deep breaths and stood up, her legs still shaky as she put her clothes back on. Master offered her a glass of water, which she politely refused, so he paid her and walked her to the door.

"Why the hell were you so nice to her?" Alex asked when he came back.

Master looked at her like this was the single most stupid thing he'd ever heard.

"To keep up appearances, obviously. Do you still want to orgasm?"

Alex's heart leaped in joy.

"Yes! Of course! Please, Master, I'll do anything!"

"I sure hope so," he sneered. "Wait right here."

Master returned a couple of minutes later, toy's leash in one hand, a gun in the other. He put a single cartridge in it, spun the cylinder, and handed it to Alex.

"You're going to fuck yourself with this. Right before you orgasm, I want you to shoot. If you don't, I promise you I'll deprive you of all sensation for a year, then I'll put you down with that poison I told you about."

Alex shivered. Master knew exactly how to push her buttons. He unlocked her belt and she eagerly pushed the barrel inside her dripping cunt. The cold, hard metal contrasted beautifully with the fire she felt inside.

Toy whined and wiggled his ass in front of Master, but all he got was a kick in the guts. He whimpered, clutching his stomach, and proceeded to grind his caged cock against the table leg.

Alex moaned, her pleasure enhanced by his despair. She slammed the muzzle repeatedly into her cervix, a pleasant heat gradually creeping up on her, heightened by the thrill of fear. If the bullet went off, she wasn't positive that it would kill her, but it would, for sure, cause irreparable damage. Her orgasm was close; she knew she couldn't hold back much longer. She closed her eyes, swallowed hard, and pulled the trigger.

Nothing happened.

She fell to her knees, shaken by a powerful

orgasm. Part of her wished that the gun had actually fired and ripped apart her insides.

"Good girl. I think you even deserve a second one as a reward."

"Thank you, Master!" she panted.

Master attached a thick double-sided dildo to toy's ring gag. One end went deep into toy's throat, almost causing him to throw up.

"Go ahead, my dear little cumrag," Master mocked, "fuck your dirty whore of a Mistress while I fuck you."

Alex spread her legs and toy crawled toward her, enthusiastically shoving the dildo inside her swollen pussy. Alex gasped in pleasure and grabbed his long hair with both hands, simulating head-handles to fuck herself energetically. Master joined them and took toy from behind. The sudden intrusion caused his legs to tremble like the previous time, but he didn't struggle or try to move away. Instead, he groaned into his gag and moved his ass in sync with Master's thrusts, desperately tugging at his cage with the vain hope of freeing his abused cock. Alex reveled in his despair and her own overpowering sense of fullness. Soon, a new orgasm hit her like a freight train and her grip on toy's hair tightened further, drawing a yelp from him. He yelped again when Master came inside him with a final, brutal thrust.

Alex patted toy's cheek as he shook, curled up on his side, fighting to catch his breath through his nose with the dildo still stuck in his throat, and struggling frantically against his cage.

"Poor plaything. You didn't get what you wanted?"

Master sneered and kicked him in the crotch.

"I wonder how long he'll last until he loses his mind completely. Or maybe he already has? I've never given this aphrodisiac to someone over a long period and without letting them feel relief."

Toy whimpered pathetically, looking at them with pleading, hazy eyes. Alex had the impression that part of him was aware of what was going on, but that he was lost in a fog of hyperarousal that pushed this spark of lucidity to the very bottom of his distorted mind, leaving him powerless to resist lust.

Kinky.

6. Christina VS the Masked Men

Alex stretched lazily, kneeling on the floor. Master was sitting on the sofa next to her watching TV, his feet resting on toy's back. Their personal slave was drooling out of his ring gag, on all fours, rubbing his legs together.

All in all, it was a nice evening. Alex hadn't been forced to put her chastity belt on, and if Master hadn't decided to hurt her more just yet, she was at least allowed to enjoy herself while witnessing toy's misery.

The doorbell rang and Master stood up with a grunt, shoving toy away with his foot.

"Stay here and don't make a noise, understood?"

"Yes, Master," Alex said.

Toy just stared at him, drooling, but he had been eager to obey any order, especially since Master had pumped him full of aphrodisiacs, so they knew they had no reason to worry about him. A couple of minutes later, Master came back with

Elias, dragging an unconscious woman behind them. The first word that came to Alex's mind when she saw her was *thicc*. She had black curly hair shaved on one side with a touch of red dye, beige skin, a cute face with large glasses, a couple of nose and ear piercings, and was dressed in blue scrubs.

"Are you sure nobody saw you?" Master asked, sounding annoyed.

"Yes, Matt, I am entirely sure. How dumb do you think I am?"

"You could have at least called. What if I had someone over?"

"With your two fucktoys here? Of course you didn't have anyone over. Now stop complaining and let's have fun!"

Elias took out two masks from his bag, one depicting a demon's face, the other a skull.

"She didn't see my face. I thought it might be fun to wear them; it would add a little spice, you know? She doesn't know what's going on, why she's here, or who we are."

Master shrugged.

"I'm not sure it'll make any real difference at this point, but sure, why not? She's your prey after all. So, what do you have in mind?"

Ɫ⫝̸⟩

They stripped and then tied up the woman—Christina—in the basement. Toy's leash was attached to a radiator, and Alex was kneeling beside him, ready to enjoy the show. At Elias's request, he and Master were shirtless with tight-fitting pants, revealing their muscular torsos and well-defined asses. Master wore the demon mask and Elias, the skull mask. Alex suspected it was a kink thing for Elias, but hey, she wasn't one to judge.

Christina woke up to the two men facing her.

"Oh, hell no!" she groaned, struggling against her restraints. "Look, I normally wouldn't say no to a pair of hot masked men, but I'm too busy for this bullshit right now."

"You're a feisty one, aren't you?" Elias laughed, pushing a gag into her mouth. "Too bad, I prefer them quiet."

Christina gave him a disdainful look and shook her head, no doubt hurling a cutting remark at him, although the exact words were erased by the gag. Alex liked her.

"Just relax," Elias purred. "We're going to make you feel really good."

He ran his hand up her leg, stopping right before reaching her cunt. Master took her breasts in his hands and rubbed her nipples between his thumb and index finger. Her body tensed, a small moan escaping her lips. Elias brushed her pussy with his slender fingers, teasing her clit until she was dripping wet. He pushed two fingers from his other hand deep inside her, causing her to gasp when he reached her G-spot. Her moans grew increasingly louder until both men abruptly stopped all stimulation. Christina looked at them, perplexed.

Elias grabbed a drill, shoved it inside her cunt,

He automatically started lapping at her drenched cunt, sending waves of ecstasy through her. She pressed his nose and mouth hard against her, making sure he couldn't breathe, and delighted in his hopeless struggle for air, her eyes fixed on the carnage that was taking place in front of her. An earth-shattering orgasm hit her and she let toy go, laughing as he coughed and panted.

ᒪᕕᒐ

Alex was very proud of toy. This time, he'd barely gagged when cleaning up the mess.

"Why don't you hide the bodies?" she asked Master as she dragged the bag to his car, Garbage following close behind. "The cops always find them. Shouldn't you . . . I don't know . . . bury them in a forest? Or hack them into tiny pieces and take them to the waste disposal center or some shit?"

"What would be the fun in that?" Master replied. "I want people to see them. Imagine the face of the little old lady or the nice jogger who falls nose to nose with a woman whose arm is sticking out of her cunt. And the family who will identify the body with the busted eye. And of course, the cops who have all these elements but are still unable to find me. It's all part of the thrill."

Alex nodded. Yeah, it made a lot of sense. Garbage rubbed her blood-covered muzzle against her leg, then took off into the bushes. She smiled, thinking about how much better her life had become since she met Master.

7. What Comes after Death? A Necrophiliac

Alex looked at the naked man bound in the basement. Master hadn't lied when he said he wanted to make the most of his time off. Barely a day after killing Christina, he had already taken Alex with him to go and catch a new victim. This time, it was a young man named Diego, who couldn't have been more than twenty, with slicked-back black hair, pale skin, dark circles under his ice-blue eyes, and a slightly demented look on his face when he was conscious.

He reminded Alex a little of a vampire on drugs. Master had taken a risk by capturing him in a small alley near the Cornavin train station, but no one had seen them.

Diego opened his eyes and immediately scowled at them defiantly. He didn't seem afraid or confused, just incredibly angry. To be fair, he had already seemed angry when they found him, and

Alex thought he was about to jump on her before Master arrived with the soporific cloth. It was hot as hell.

"What the fuck do you want with me, you fuckers?" Diego spat. "If you're expecting a ransom, you're going to be disappointed. Do I really look like someone anyone gives a shit about?"

"No, you do not." Master smiled, almost kindly. "And believe me, that is very convenient for us."

"You're that fucking serial killer," Diego stated almost matter-of-factly. He suddenly seemed to register that he was naked, that Alex was wearing extremely revealing clothes, and that toy was leashed to a piece of furniture, drooling and tugging at his caged crotch. He grinned hatefully and spread his legs. "Oh, so you're going to fucking rape and murder me? Go ahead, do your worst. I'm not scared of some pussy-ass wannabe Jack the Ripper."

Alex laughed. She liked this one too. He was fun. Master, on the other hand, didn't seem

with one brutal push. The young man's eyes widened and his legs shook, but he kept them open and his sneer barely faltered. Alex was surprised to see that his dick was still limp; he sure did look like he enjoyed it. Maybe he had erectile problems?

Master pressed a button at the base of the object and Diego gasped as a high-voltage electric shock passed through his body. Master pressed again, and Diego let out a scream that sounded more like a gurgle. A third shock and he finally pressed his legs together, his grin replaced by a grimace of pure agony. A fourth shock. He shook his head adamantly, trying to beg despite his cut-out tongue. A fifth shock. He was now in tears, trembling and covered in sweat. A charred smell was spreading through the room.

Master pulled the object out of the man's anus, ripping off a layer of burnt skin in the process.

"Now that's better." He smiled and unzipped his pants, satisfied.

Diego looked at him pleadingly, all bravado gone. Master forced his legs apart once again and slid inside him slowly, purposefully rubbing against his raw walls. Diego had turned ashen and thrashed fruitlessly against his bonds. His breathing was ragged, each of Master's thrusts further ravaging his scorched insides. Much to Alex's surprise, he still wasn't hard. Weird.

Master held out his hand and Alex gave him his scalpel without hesitation. She knew that, for some reason, he preferred it to the knife.

He punctured Diego's lower abdomen and deliberately slashed through it, opening a gaping wound from which slimy viscera oozed. Master continued cutting until he had removed a large circle of flesh, leaving the guts fully on display. He held Diego's head down, forcing him to watch his intestine bulge and move back and forth as he fucked him. Alex wasn't sure whether he died before or after Master climaxed, but in any case, it was a gorgeous sight.

Master pulled out and severed the large intestine at the rectum. He untied toy's leash from the furniture, guided him to the body, and removed his cage. Toy's cock instantly sprang up, swollen with need.

"I'm in a generous mood today. Enjoy."

Toy didn't need to be told twice. He threw himself at the corpse and buried his shaft into the disconnected hole. Alex laughed as she watched him hump the cadaver while his dick poked at its organs through the opening. It was only a matter of seconds before he came, spilling his cum among the viscera. For a brief moment, his eyes filled with horrified lucidity and he stepped back, but Master put his cage back on and teased his ass, and soon the haze of lust filled his gaze once again.

"What about me?" Alex asked eagerly.

"I'm glad you brought it up," Master replied, grabbing her wrists and trapping her in his strong hold. "This little arrangement was intriguing for a while, but I'm getting rather tired of it. I have decided that the time has come for me to kill you."

Alex's heart leaped with joy, her lower abdomen filling with a wonderful heat.

"Don't get your hopes up." Master smiled

wickedly. "Remember that poison I told you about? That's how I'm going to do it. Most of my victims would beg for such a sweet, painless death, but for you, it's the cruelest thing I could do. You have no idea how hard it makes me denying you of your dreams."

"But . . . you promised . . ." Alex shook her head in bewilderment, unable to free herself from Master's grip. Tears welled up in her eyes.

"And you really believed I gave a shit about you? Poor naive little whore."

Master pulled a syringe from his pocket. Panic-stricken, Alex struggled with all her strength. She didn't want to go out like that. Anything but that. It felt like the world was crumbling beneath her feet. Suddenly, Master let out a pained gasp and loosened his grip slightly, just enough for Alex to free herself. She reached for the knife, still stained with Diego's blood, and plunged it deep into Master's chest. He opened his mouth in surprise, but only a trickle of blood came out. Gently, as if in slow motion, he fell to his knees, holding his hand out weakly toward her. Alex couldn't tell whether he was trying to caress her cheek or strangle her, but it made no difference either way. His strength was failing him fast. He fell onto his side, the syringe slipping from his hand and rolling to the floor. His chest was still rising and falling slightly, but it was clear he wasn't going to get up again. A furry little muzzle nudged against Alex's leg and she knelt down to pet Garbage gratefully.

"Thank you, girl. You're the best. Look at you, you bit off a whole chunk of his leg! Eat all you want. You've earned it. Good girl."

The little possum didn't hesitate. She headed for the hole she'd already made in Master's leg— *Matt's* leg, the bastard didn't deserve the honorific—and continued nibbling, tearing off little pieces of flesh and holding them in her tiny paws before swallowing them hungrily. Matt groaned and tried to move his leg to chase her away, but his strength had already left him.

Alex was glad he wasn't quite dead yet. It made

what she had in mind that much more interesting. She straddled his chest and positioned the knife handle against her aching cunt, then lowered herself brutally, allowing the whole handle to penetrate her. It felt good, but what felt even better was Matt's bulging eyes and the choked moans he let out every time she pushed the knife deeper into him. It was like using a double-sided dildo, but way, way hotter. She stroked her swollen clit while the handle pressed on her G-spot. The light finally went out in Matt's eyes and his head lolled to one side. That pushed her over the edge, her orgasm hitting her like an electric shock that left her panting, her legs shaking.

She gave herself a few moments to catch her breath, then headed for the shower without looking back. She sighed with contentment as the steaming water poured over her body. Now that Matt was dead, she had to think about what she was going to do. Of course she could just go home and pretend like nothing had happened, or even report him to the cops. No one would suspect her of anything other than killing a serial killer in self-defense, but now that she'd tasted blood, she didn't want to stop.

By the time she emerged from the shower, a plan had formed in her mind.

8. Embracing the Predator

Alex went back down to the cellar and arranged the two corpses in such a way as to give the impression that they had killed each other. Once she was satisfied, she grabbed a still-leashed toy who was drooling in one corner, called Garbage, and went back up to the living room. She took all the money from Matt's wallet, as well as his car keys and her phone, stuffed toy into the trunk, and took the wheel.

She stopped at her apartment to pick up some of her belongings, which she piled into the trunk on top of toy, and set off again. After driving for a couple of hours with Garbage curled up comfortably in her lap, she reached the end of the road she could travel by car.

She parked the black Porsche in a remote spot between the trees where she knew it would rot for years before anyone found it. Garbage jumped out, happy to stretch her cute little legs, and ran in a circle around her. Alex took toy out of the trunk and grabbed her belongings, then set off walking along the secluded mountain path. Toy, still on a leash, crawled behind her while Garbage ran back and forth excitedly. If anyone had seen them, they'd have been more than a little shocked, but Alex knew that no one ever came here. The only place this road led to was her family's old chalet, in which no one had been interested for as long as she could remember. It would be the perfect place to continue exploring her passion at her discretion. She could kidnap hikers and have fun with them, and the garden would give her everything she needed. Except for meat, of course, but the hikers would supply that. And if she needed to go into town, there was a bus stop about two hours away. What more could she ask for?

Toy whimpered behind her, his palms and knees battered by the rocky path. She considered killing him, but she'd grown attached, and it would be nice to have some company. They finally reached the chalet. It was in a sorry state but still habitable, and fixing it up would be a nice way to spend her time between victims. She attached toy's leash to the old doghouse at the back of the garden. It would make a perfect home for him when she didn't want to play with him. Toy looked at her with desperate eyes, and she had the impression he wanted to talk to her but the ring gag prevented him from forming coherent sounds. She shrugged and went inside.

She called Garbage, "Come, girl! I'll show you around. I'll set up your own comfy little bed next to mine, and you can come and go as you please and eat all the human flesh you want. You'll see, it will be awesome! We'll have to stray a bit from home to hunt, but I know exactly where to find plenty of hikers. And if you want a little treat when we don't have any on hand, there's always toy."

Alex laughed gleefully as she imagined the future that awaited her. It felt so good to finally embrace her inner predator.

The End of Book One

About the Author

Aiden E. Messer does not exist. Are they an illusion, a ghost, a mere thought? No one knows. If we are to believe one of the children they seem to work with, if they were a teacher, they would be as tall as a human. They are not a teacher. According to various sources, they have studied psychology and have always had a penchant for horror and the macabre. They like to combine these subjects in their books.

Thank you so much for reading!

If you enjoyed this weird little book, don't forget to review it on Goodreads, StoryGraph, Godless, Amazon, etc. I would really appreciate it!

Aiden E. Messer

Printed in Great Britain
by Amazon

48575963R10056